THE ARTHUR BOOKS

BUFFALO ARTHUR
THE LONE ARTHUR
ARTHUR THE KID
RAILROAD ARTHUR
KLONDIKE ARTHUR
ARTHUR'S LAST STAND

THIS PAPERBACK EDITION FIRST PUBLISHED
IN GREAT BRITAIN IN 1978 BY ROBSON BOOKS
LTD., 28 POLAND STREET, LONDON W1V 3DB.
ORIGINALLY PUBLISHED IN HARDBACK BY
ROBSON BOOKS IN 1976. COPYRIGHT © 1976
ALAN COREN.

Coren, Alan
Buffalo Arthur. – (Coren, Alan. Arthur books).
I. Title
823′.9′1J   PZ7.C/

ISBN 0 86051 023 9 paperback
     0 903895 75 7 hardback

Printed in Hungary by Kossuth Printing House, Budapest

ALAN COREN
BUFFALO ARTHUR

Illustrated by JOHN ASTROP

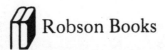
Robson Books

For Deborah and Manuela

Once upon a time, about a hundred years ago, in the Far West of America, in the very middle of a rather awful place called Arizona Territory, there was a ranch.

Of course, Arizona wasn't awful for everybody. Very few places are awful for everybody. Arizona, for example, was just the place to be if you were a rattlesnake. You could guess that from the name of the place, because Arizona means The Dry Country in Spanish, and when the first Spanish explorers crossed the Far West and wanted to think up names for the places they went through to put on their maps, The Dry Country was the first thing they thought of to call it.

And it was precisely *because* it was dry that rattlesnakes liked it. They liked to lie in the hot yellow-grey dust, or slither in and out of the yellow-grey rocks, and because they were yellow-grey, too, their enemies could not see them. And the animals they preyed on for food couldn't see them either: if you were a desert rat, one moment you might be passing a dusty stick, and the next moment the dusty stick would have eaten you, because it wasn't a dusty stick at all, but a rattlesnake.

Arizona was also just the place if you were a Gila monster, or a tarantula spider, or a scorpion; which is why I think of Arizona as rather awful, because all those animals are poisonous, and not really my favourite animals at all.

Mind you, Arizona was, and is, very beautiful indeed; and if you could just look at it without worrying about snakes, spiders, scorpions, Gila monsters and so on, you would be right to think that it wasn't awful but very exciting: its mountains soar up from its vast yellow deserts, and at sunset its skies seem to catch fire, blazing orange and crimson and gold, fading at last to the colour of darkening plums before blackening into the blackest night you could ever imagine, so black that the stars seem not just white, but brilliant silver.

And it was in the very middle of all this, the hot yellow skies by day and the cold black skies by night, that the ranch stood that was called the Dusty D.

It was called the Dusty D because – well, you know by now why it was called Dusty, and the D came from the name of the man who built it, and that name was Dan Dundee. He had been a soldier in the American Civil War, and when the War had ended in 1865 he had ridden away from the battlefields in search of somewhere quiet and peaceful, somewhere where he wouldn't have to see people, because it had been a very terrible war indeed, and Dan Dundee had decided that he would like to be on his own for a while in a silent empty place. And he rode for a thousand miles and more, west from Tennessee, through Arkansas and Oklahoma Territory, through Texas and New Mexico, until he came at last to the hot quiet flatlands of Arizona, where, just because he liked it (which is a very good reason, after all), he stopped.

And he built a one-roomed cabin in a place where there was a little creek, and he irrigated a small patch of land with water from the creek, and grass grew from the moistened sandy soil; and Dan Dundee worked very hard for five years, and at the end of five years the Dusty D wasn't quite so dusty, and he had a hundred cattle on his fairly green land. And partly because his ranch was now growing bigger quite rapidly, and partly because after five years he was beginning to feel he would like to have some people to talk to again, he decided to take on two men to be ranch-hands, who would help with the five hundred cattle he planned to buy as soon as he had the men to look after them.

So he saddled his horse, and he rode sixty miles, across the scrublands, over the Rio Verde, and through the hills at the foot of the Vulture Mountains until he came to the little town of Buckeye Bend, which wasn't much more than a church and a wooden hotel and a saloon and a general store and a livery stable and a gunsmith's and a barber shop and twenty-two little wooden houses where the people of Buckeye Bend sat and wondered how long it would take the railroad company to build a line to Buckeye Bend. Because until the railroad got there, Buckeye Bend would remain remarkably unimportant, and nobody likes living in a remarkably unimportant place.

The railroad company kept promising; but nothing seemed to happen.

Well, anyway, Dan Dundee got down from his horse, and gave it to the man at the livery stable to groom and feed, and he walked across to the wooden hotel and asked for the best room and he got the one with the washbasin in it, and he washed and cleaned his teeth and he brushed the yellow-grey Arizona dust from his clothes and he combed his hair, and he went downstairs and ordered two steaks in the dining room.

You may think that sounds greedy, you may feel that Dan Dundee was, not to put too fine a point on it, a bit of a pig; but you have to remember that in 1870 it took nearly two days to ride sixty miles, and Dan Dundee had missed two dinners, not to mention two lunches, so it was only reasonable, really, to want two steaks.

And he enjoyed his meal very much, except that the waiter dropped a potato into his lap and spilled beer onto his boots.

Which prompted Dan Dundee, who was quite a polite man, all in all, to say:

"Excuse me, but how long have you been a waiter?"

To which the waiter replied:

"I started this morning. They used to have a real waiter here, but he got sick and tired of

waiting for the railroad to come, so he rode off last night. I'm a cowhand, but the man I worked for went out last week without his boots, and a scorpion got him in the foot, so that was that."

And Dan Dundee said:

"There's a coincidence! I happen to be in town looking for a couple of cowhands, how'd you like to come and work for me?"

The waiter took off his apron.

"When can I start?" he said.

"It's a long ride," warned Dan Dundee, "and hard work when you get there."

"Anything's better than waiting tables," said the ex-waiter. "I'm covered in soup, and I've only served three people so far. Also, I think the cook has roasted my hat."

"What?" said Dan Dundee.

"I hung it next to the stove this morning," explained the ex-waiter, "and now it's disappeared, and there's a strange smell coming from the oven. I looked inside, and there was something that looked very much like my hat, with carrots round it."

"Lucky for you I happened along," said Dan Dundee (who was secretly hoping his steaks *had* been steaks, rather than shoes or table mats, or something), and he finished his beer, and the two men walked out of the hotel and into the yellow-grey-dusty street.

There was nobody about.

"I wonder," said Dan Dundee, "where I'll find another cowhand."

"I don't know," said the ex-waiter, whose name was Billy Futt. "Everyone's indoors worrying about the railroad."

"Have you got a horse?" asked Dan Dundee.

"He's over in the livery stable," said Billy Futt.

They went through the great wooden doors of San Sundown's Livery Stable, into the smell of leather and horse and hay. Sam Sundown himself came out of the horsey dark to meet them. He held the reins of their two horses.

"Last horses I'll ever do," he said, a little sadly.

"How come?" said Dan Dundee.

"When the railroad comes," said the farrier, "the stagecoach will close down, and without the stagecoach horses to care for, I just won't be able to survive."

Dan Dundee looked at the yellow sky, narrowing his eyes against the fearful brass glare, and thought for a bit.

"How would you like," he said at last, "to be a cowboy?"

Which is why, at two o'clock in the afternoon of August the ninth, 1870, three men rode out of Buckeye Bend, turned sharp left at the church, and took the trail that led to the Dusty D.

For the next five years, everyone worked incredibly hard.

They dug more irrigation ditches so that more land could be watered and more grass grown and more cattle put onto the grass to feed and be sold for more money to buy more tools to build more irrigation ditches and more wire to put up more fences to keep in more cattle. They built a bunkhouse onto the ranch-house and a cookhouse onto the bunkhouse and a wash-house onto the cookhouse.

Now, because the three cowboys worked so hard, they slept very deeply indeed. At the end of the day, they would have just enough energy left to eat their suppers of steaks, eggs, beans, fried potatoes, sweet corn, and deep-dish apple pie, and to wash themselves and clean their teeth, before tumbling from the cookhouse into the bunkhouse and falling onto their beds. They always had the same meal, by the way, because it was the only meal that Sam Sundown had ever learned to cook. But he cooked it very well indeed, having learned how to from a famous Arizona chef who had taught him to cook it in return for Sam Sundown's having removed a stone from the hoof of the chef's horse, which Sam Sundown did with a special spike on his pen-knife.

And because they slept very deeply, they did not hear anything at all during the night of September the eighteenth, 1875.

But when, in the morning, after a hearty breakfast of steaks, eggs, beans, fried potatoes, sweet corn and deep-dish apple pie, the three cowboys went out to check the fences, they became aware that something was not as it should be.

It was Billy Futt who expressed it most clearly.

"We haven't got all our cattle," he said.

They were standing on a very small hill, called a knoll, at the time; and because the land around the Dusty D was very flat, they were able to see the whole ranch.

"*I* thought that," said Sam Sundown, "only I didn't like to say."

"Let's count them," said Dan Dundee.

So they did.

It was a bit tricky, because the cattle kept moving, and as they were all about the same size and all brown with white splodges on,

they could never be sure they hadn't counted any twice. But by mid-afternoon, and after a lot of scribbling in the dust with the barrels of their six-guns, the three cowboys were generally agreed that what they had were 417 cattle.

Whereas on the day before they had had 681.

"What," asked Dan Dundee, "is 681 take away 417?"

They thought for a while. Eventually, Billy Futt, who was better than the other two at arithmetic, though not much, said:

"264."

"That's bad," said Dan Dundee. "I made it 9. If there were only 9 missing, well, you could always suppose they'd just wandered away, or fallen into the creek, or something. But not when it's 264. Do you know what's happened, in my opinion?"

"We've been robbed," said Sam Sundown.

"Nearly right," said Dan Dundee. "Rustled, is what we've been. Rustlers have come in the night and gone off with 264 of our cattle!" And as he said this, his lips were tight, and his jaw was set, and his fists were clenched, and his eyes were bright with anger. He was thinking of all the work, all the ditching, all the fencing, all the hard days of riding and roping and branding, and he was thinking of the rustlers who had done none of this but had merely crept up in the night and taken what was not theirs to take, and ridden off again. "When I get hold of those men," said Dan Dundee, in a dangerously quiet voice, "I will . . ."

He did not finish, because the things that he was thinking of doing were so terrible, he could not even bring himself to mention them.

"But how," said Sam Sundown, who was the most practical of the three, "shall we catch up with them? You have to know all sorts of stuff, like how to track, and how to stalk, and, er . . ."

"How to surround," said Billy Futt, who had heard tales on other ranches. "You have to know how to *surround* rustlers. Also," and here he went rather pale, "you have to be able to shoot them. I'm not sure I fancy that. Tin cans and targets and rabbits are one thing, but people, well . . ."

"It's a job," said Dan Dundee, who had suddenly realised the problems, too, despite his anger, "for the Sheriff. We must ride down to Buckeye Bend!"

So he and Sam Sundown, leaving Billy Futt to guard the ranch and the remaining cattle (a job which he was proud to do, though understandably nervous, it being even worse than waiting on tables), put on their best chaps and jackets, and set off once again for Buckeye Bend.

"Not a hope," said the Sheriff. He was tall, and lean, and wore a long black coat, cut-away to leave his black holsters and their black-handled revolvers clear, and looked more than a match for any ten rustlers; but still he shook his head.

"Whyever not?" cried Dan Dundee.

"It's your job!" exclaimed Sam Sundown.

"Nope," said the Sheriff, "it ain't." And he leaned back in his swivel chair, and he put his black boots on his leather-topped desk, and he pointed his black-gloved hand past the rows of rifles, past the doors of the cells, and out of his office window towards the street outside. "Buckeye Bend," he said, "is a big town now."

It was. Dan Dundee and Sam Sundown had noticed that. Indeed, they had almost fallen out of their saddles at the sight of the hundreds of buildings, and the many streets, the dozen new saloons, the hotels with five floors, the smart shops, the four churches, the opera house, and most of all, of course, at the sight of the railway station. For the railroad had come, at last, to Buckeye Bend; and Buckeye Bend was *somewhere* now, and the people wore fine clothes, and there was a dance every month.

"It may be a big town, all right," said Dan Dundee, "but I don't see why that stops you from going after rustlers."

The Sheriff flicked a speck of cigar-ash from his elegant black sleeve. When he looked at the two cowboys, yellow-grey-dusted from the trail, he had something in his eyes which was very like a sneer.

"I don't do cheap stuff," he said. "I deal with bank robberies – we have *three* banks in Buckeye Bend now, you know – and famous gunslingers who have their faces on real printed posters, and big-time gamblers, and men who hold up trains, and gangs of gold-thieves known from coast to coast. I don't," he said, "have time for mere cattle-thieves."

"But what can we *do*?" cried Dan Dundee.

The Sheriff stood up, and took down his elegant black hat from its peg, and put it on carefully, and examined it in the mirror.

"Try putting an ad in the paper," he said. "It's a pretty important paper these days, the *Buckeye Bugle.*"

And, giving his fine moustache a final twirl, he went out.

The two cowboys followed him into the street. By coincidence, the newspaper office was bang opposite. They walked across, and went in, and asked for a piece of paper and a pencil.

Dan Dundee licked the pencil.

"It ought to say WANTED at the top," he said.

"Good," said Sam Sundown, "I like that. It gets you off on the right foot immediately."

"Wanted," wrote Dan Dundee, spelling carefully, "someone who can track down ruslers quick."

"I think," said Sam Sundown, "there's a 't' in rustlers."

Dan Dundee wrote it in.

"And you ought to have something about getting the cattle back again."

Dan Dundee licked his pencil once more. He wrote. He cleared his throat.

"Wanted," he read, "someone who can track down rustlers quick, also get cattle back, top prices paid for right man, plus good food including steaks, apply Dusty D ranch, near Buckeye Bend, Arizona."

"I like that," said Sam Sundown.

So they handed it to the man behind the counter. He looked at it.

"That word ought to be 'quickly' not 'quick'," he said. "Don't you cowboys know *anything*?"

Out on the street, Sam Sundown said:

"I'm not sure I like Buckeye Bend as much as I did."

"I know what you mean," said Dan Dundee.

Back at the ranch, six days passed.

Every morning, the cowboys leapt from their bunks to see if the postman had called (he only came by once a week, since they were so far from anywhere, but they didn't know which day he came, because none of them had ever received a letter), and every day they crept back disappointed to the cookhouse for breakfast.

But on the seventh day, there was a knock on the door, and a postman on the mat, handing them a white envelope!

"At long last!" cried Billy Futt, which was what they all felt.

Dan Dundee tore open the envelope, and unfolded the letter.

"Dear cowboys of the Dusty D," he read, "I saw your advertisement and you could not have come to a better man. I will capture the rustlers and get your cattle back in a flash. Please meet me at Buckeye Bend station next Tuesday, I shall be arriving on the two o'clock train, signed Yours till the cows come home (ha! ha!) ... "

"Well, go on!" cried Sam Sundown, "Who is it?"

Dan Dundee had gone very white.

"It's signed," he whispered, "Buffalo Bill!"

The other two gasped

"What a stroke of luck!" said Billy Futt.

"And," said Dan Dundee, "he spelled 'rustlers' right."

On the following Monday, Dan Dundee and Billy Futt (for it was his turn this time) set off, in their best clothes, for Buckeye Bend, and by Tuesday lunchtime they were riding down the main street towards the station.

"Half-past one," said Dan Dundee, glancing at the smart station clock as they dismounted and tethered their horses.

Far off, a whistle blew, echoing.

"That'll be the two o'clock train," said Billy Futt, who was so excited he had to put both hands on his head to stop them shaking.

They watched the train grow from a distant dot beneath a plume of black smoke until, at last, it pulled, hissing and clanging and grunting, to a stop in front of them, filling the station with reek and thunder, a great orange barrel, hooped with gold bands, the black cab as high, it seemed, as the station roof, an iron giant that drove their horses' ears against their heads in terror. It was quite simply the biggest moving thing that either of them had ever seen.

The passengers started to disembark. As Buckeye Bend was the end of the line, there were few aboard. Twelve people got down: two old ladies with a caged green parrot, four cowhands laughing, two troopers in blue uniforms, an Indian guide in buckskins, a young woman with a baby, and last of all, a small boy of about seven wearing spectacles and carrying an orange carpet-bag.

The two cowboys craned and peered.

"I've seen his picture," said Dan Dundee. "He's tall, with a yellow beard, wears high boots and an elk-skin hat with a Pawnee feather in it."

The passengers passed them one by one.

The guard waved his flag.

The train-whistle blew, and slowly the huge thing shunted off into a siding.

There was nobody left on the platform at all.

"He must have missed it," muttered Dan Dundee.

"Um," said Billy Futt.

They were so disappointed, they could not even move.

It was as they were standing miserably there that a voice behind them, low down, said:

"Excuse me, but are you the cowboys from the Dusty D?"

They turned. The small boy was looking up at them.

"That's us," said Dan Dundee. "Why?"

"How do you do?" said the little boy. He held out his hand. "I'm Buffalo Bill."

There was a very long silence.

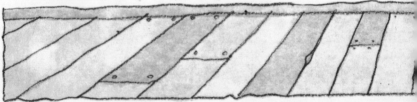

"Buffalo Bill," said Billy Futt at last, "is nearly seven feet tall. Apart from anything else, such as beards."

"That's the other one," said the boy. "I didn't say I was *the* Buffalo Bill, did I? Lots of people have the same name. Look at all the Smiths there are."

"*You* are called Buffalo Bill?" said Dan Dundee, who had clutched at Billy Futt to keep from falling down in astonishment.

"Well," said the boy, "Bill is actually my middle name. I am Arthur William Foskett. Strictly speaking, I suppose, I ought to start calling myself Buffalo Arthur. To avoid confusion."

"It would certainly help," said Billy Futt. "We were expecting someone a bit, er, older."

'I'm seven," said Buffalo Arthur. "You can't get a lot older than that."

Dan Dundee drew Billy Futt aside.

"What can we do with him?" he muttered. "There's not another train out of here for three days. We can't just leave a kid hanging around in Buckeye Bend."

"We'll take him back to the ranch, feed him up, and send him back in a few days' time," said Billy Futt. "No other choice."

"Come on, kid," said Dan Dundee, "let's head for the Dusty D."

"You mean I'm hired?" said Buffalo Arthur. "That's great!"

Billy Futt sighed.

"Ride up here with me," he said.

And off they went.

Sam Sundown was a bit surprised, but he had
been brought up to be polite, so made no
reference to Buffalo Arthur's size. He had
never seen any pictures of Buffalo Bill, so had
not known what to expect, anyway.

They all sat down to a meal of steaks, eggs,
beans, fried potatoes, sweet corn, and deep-
dish apple pie, but nobody could think of very
much to say. This was because the three cowboys were all too disappointed by the fact that
instead of Buffalo Bill they had ended up with
Buffalo Arthur, and because Buffalo Arthur
himself, tired out from the journey, had fallen
asleep with his face in the pie-dish.

So they carried him to the bunkhouse, and
they put him in the most comfortable bunk,
and they sighed for a bit, and then Billy Futt
blew out the light, and they all fell asleep.

The Arizona dawn came up, pale gold pushing back the blue-edged black of night, spilling its yellowness into the bunkhouse, falling across the sleeping faces, warming them, nudging them, finally waking them.

It was Billy Futt who was first up.

He stretched. He yawned. He scratched. He might have been a huge cat in a red flannel nightshirt.

And then, his eyes having been duly rubbed, Billy Futt stared.

He woke Dan Dundee and Sam Sundown.

They all stared.

For where Buffalo Arthur had lain only the night before, there was now nothing but the faint dent his little body had made upon the mattress.

They ran into the cookhouse, but he wasn't there. He wasn't in the ranch-house, either, nor the wash-house. They ran off in three different directions shouting "ARTHUR! ARTHUR!" but no sound came back, save the mooing of the irritated cattle, or the neigh of a startled horse.

"Gone!" cried Dan Dundee.

"Vanished!" cried Sam Sundown.

"Disappeared!" cried Billy Futt.

None of them knew what to do. They had small experience of little boys, and did not have the first idea of where to look for them when they disappeared.

Few grown-ups do.

So they simply sat down for breakfast, hoping that something would occur to them. But, for the first time ever, they could not manage their steaks, nor their eggs, nor their beans, nor their fried potatoes, nor their sweet corn, nor even their deep-dish apple pie.

"He was our responsibility," said Dan Dundee, pushing his untouched plate away.

"He didn't know the West," muttered Billy Futt. "He may have woken up in the night, gone for a walk, and been got."

They all knew what he meant by "got".

Apart from rattlers, Gila monsters, tarantulas and scorpions, there were all sorts of animals, from coyotes to mountain lions, that tended to wander about Arizona, getting you.

The three cowboys, though there were fences to be mended, and cattle to be tended, and a hundred other chores to be done, sat at the table until the sun was high in the sky, not moving.

Occasionally, Billy Futt would say: "I'll go back to waiting tables" or Sam Sundown would say: "I'll find me a livery stable somewhere" or Dan Dundee would say: "I shall close down the ranch and sell the cattle and go back to Tennessee and open a sweetshop and give all the sweets away to children", and everyone knew why they were all saying these things, but it didn't make them feel any better, not the least little bit.

They need not have worried. For Buffalo Arthur had not been got at all. In fact, it was Buffalo Arthur who did the getting.

The night before, when the three cowboys were snoring in their beds and dreaming cowboy dreams, Buffalo Arthur, who had only been pretending to be asleep, slid very carefully and very quietly from his bunk. Holding his boots, and tiptoeing cautiously across the creaky floorboards, he passed like a shadow between the other bunks, and out of the bunkhouse door.

Outside, Buffalo Arthur shivered. Not just because it was suddenly cold – Arizona nights can be as cold as the days are hot – but because of what he knew he had to do. And it was the sort of night that would have made anyone shiver, even if they weren't cold and even if they didn't have anything shivery to do.

For the moon was high and silver-bright, and strong moonlight robs everything of its colour; so that all around Buffalo Arthur the ranch-buildings and the grassy slopes and the animals and the cactus and the far hills were all painted in shades of cold bluey-grey, and all the shadows cast were hard and black, and Buffalo Arthur could never be quite sure when something was a shadow and when it was not. He put on his boots, and stepped with great care and concentration: that black shape might be a cactus shadow, or it might be a deadly rattlesnake, that black blob might be a rock, or a lethal spider waiting to scuttle out and get him, that black pool might . . .

Somewhere, a coyote howled, a terrible echoing wail, chill as the night, making the small hairs prickle on Buffalo Arthur's neck and reminding him of how far he had to go and how little he knew of what might happen along the way. But he clenched his teeth, and he squared his shoulders, and he walked on, because he was very brave.

If you wanted to call yourself Buffalo anything, you had to be.

For perhaps half an hour, he walked all around the area close to the ranch, looking, examining, calculating, sometimes dropping on all fours to peer more closely, sometimes climbing high up to gaze out over the silent countryside, until he spotted the clue he was seeking. And when he spotted it, he did not hesitate; he walked quickly down to the corral, and he threw a saddle over a little pony who had been quietly standing there asleep, not realising that he would have work to do that night, and rode out through the gates of the Dusty D.

For two hours, Buffalo Arthur rode, as quickly as he dared on this unfamiliar track, pausing here and there to check for the signs that would tell him he was still going in the right direction: a broken bush here, a trampled field there, the odd cactus with its spines worn smooth where something large and thick-skinned had rubbed past it, and as he cantered on, so the signs grew clearer and made a pattern in his head; and Buffalo Arthur knew that he had been right, all along.

Suddenly, the trail forked. Buffalo Arthur reined in, and considered: one track led off into the flat scrubland lying like grey pumice-stone beneath the chill moon; one track went off in the other direction, disappearing into a black gully between two huge dark hills. Buffalo Arthur dismounted, and knelt to examine the ground. Above him, his pony whinnied and snorted, steam rising from his flanks, his eyes white as the moon itself, and rolling nervously. The pony was no happier about the night's doings than Buffalo Arthur, and who could blame either of them?

Especially as Buffalo Arthur suddenly saw what he had been seeking, and realised that it meant they would have to take the trail that led between the hills and into the pitch-black shadow of the valley!

But after he had ridden a little way, slowly, and as quietly as he could (for he knew that he was very close, now), the blackness was suddenly not quite so black.

There was a tiny orange flicker in the distance, perhaps a half-mile or so off; it was hard, at night, to tell exactly. And when he saw it, Buffalo Arthur's heart jumped inside him, and his mouth went so dry he couldn't swallow.

He got down, and tethered the pony to a tree.

He would have to do this last, terrible part on foot.

It took him about fifteen minutes, during which time the orange flicker grew gradually larger, and became the camp-fire he had guessed it to be.

Buffalo Arthur, just a few yards off now, dropped to the cold ground and began to creep on his tummy, trying not to think of all the other things that might be creeping about down there in the darkness, too. Anyway, however frightening *they* were, they were nowhere near as terrifying as what he saw around the camp-fire.

There, in the pool of orange firelight, lay three of the biggest, ugliest, wickedest-looking men Buffalo Arthur had ever seen! They lay with their heads on their saddles, and their

hands on their guns: the tiniest noise, Buffalo Arthur knew, would have those heads off the saddles and those terrible guns blazing, and the thought of it fixed Buffalo Arthur to the spot as if he had been suddenly turned to stone.

But he had come so far, and he was as brave as it is possible to be, and he had no intention of giving up now and running away. Especially as, now his eyes had grown used to the darkness beyond the firelight, he was able to make out the lumpy shapes of cattle, like black boulders, standing in a great mass, making no sound.

Buffalo Arthur did not have to count them to know that there would be 264 of them there.

But what was he to do? Had he been a grown-up and wearing a gun, it might have been a different matter; though even then, there were very few grown-ups, perhaps not even Buffalo Bill himself, who would have dared to take on three such dangerous-looking villains on their own. But for a small boy, with no gun at all, it was out of the question. Should he run back to the pony, and gallop home to the Dusty D, and tell the cowboys? Impossible! The rustlers might well be gone by the time they got back, and even if they weren't, the chances were that Sam Sundown and Billy Futt and Dan Dundee would be no match at all for them, and would simply be shot to pieces.

There was no way out of it, Buffalo Arthur decided, firmly: he would have to do the job himself, alone, unarmed. After all, he told himself, he *had* applied for the job, so he ought to have known that sooner or later it might come to this. And there was one thing about which Buffalo Arthur was very certain: you did not boast about what you could do, or promise people that you would do it, if you didn't intend to go through with it.

It was when he noticed the lassoos tied to each saddle beneath each wicked head that Buffalo Arthur finally made up his mind. And having had the idea, he didn't stop to think about it, just in case the thinking made him faint at the awful possibilities of something going wrong: he just unfroze his limbs, and crawled towards the flickering flames.

It was easy enough untying the lassoos from the saddles; cowboys (or, come to that, rustlers) always kept them loosely tied in case they had to do a snappy piece of roping. With the three coils of rope in his hand, Buffalo Arthur steeled himself for the next horrifying part of his master plan!

Knots were his speciality. He knew how to tie every sort of knot there was, clove hitches and sheepshanks and double-grannies and slip-knots, because Buffalo Arthur had realised a very long time ago that knots were just about the most useful things there were, and had set out to master them. It may surprise you, but Buffalo Arthur had been able to tie his shoelaces before he was three!

And he had even invented a knot, a knot so complicated, so miraculous, that it contained the best bits of every other sort of knot there was, plus a special little twist that was Buffalo Arthur's own idea. It was the only knot there has ever been that couldn't be untied. You had to cut it instead.

He had never needed it before. Ordinary knots had always done until that moment. But if ever there was a moment when a special knot was called for, this was the one!

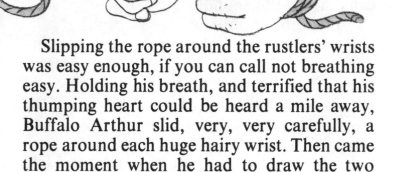

Slipping the rope around the rustlers' wrists was easy enough, if you can call not breathing easy. Holding his breath, and terrified that his thumping heart could be heard a mile away, Buffalo Arthur slid, very, very carefully, a rope around each huge hairy wrist. Then came the moment when he had to draw the two wrists of each villain together!

The first pair of wrists was no problem; the rustler lay on his back snoring, his hands together on the front of his dirty grey shirt. In a flash, Buffalo Arthur had tied firm the Special Knot!

The second pair was trickier. The rustler lay on his side, one arm in view, the other tucked under him, its hand holding the gun. Hardly believing that he was doing it, Buffalo Arthur gradually eased the arm out, his face right up against the great black-bearded snoring face of the rustler. And as Buffalo Arthur lifted the second hand towards the first – it was unbelievably heavy, like a great hairy stone, each filthy black fingernail horribly bitten to a jagged edge, more like an animal's awful claw then a human hand – the rustler stirred in his sleep!

The mouth so close to Buffalo Arthur's opened, and from behind the yellow teeth, came a terrible sound!

"Aaaargh! Shubbalubble! Wurrgh!"

It was like being close to a great gurgling drain. It was then that Buffalo Arthur, petrified as he was, smelt the stale smell of whisky, and realised, with some relief, that the rustlers had probably fallen asleep drunk, and serve them right.

He tied the second pair of hands, and laid the second gun beside the first, well out of reach, and crawled gingerly across to the last rustler.

It was while he was putting the finishing touches to the final Special Knot that the man stirred, like the first, and, without any more

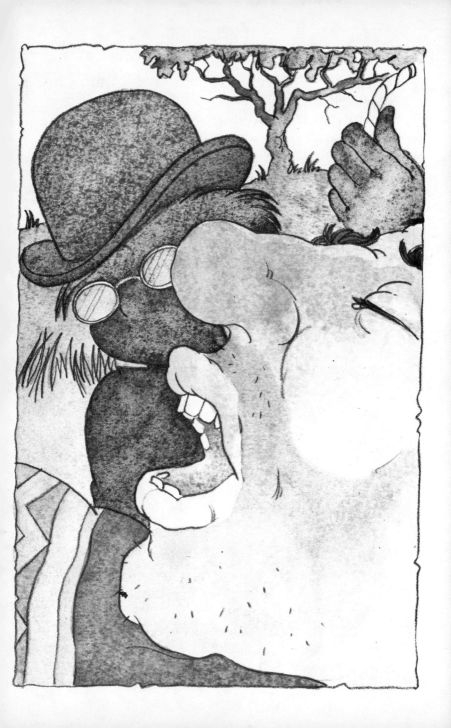

warning, suddenly rolled over onto his stomach.

With Buffalo Arthur underneath him.

It's the end, thought Buffalo Arthur, holding himself tight against the inevitable moment when the man would wake up, and roar, and roll over, and aim the gun which Buffalo Arthur had not yet managed to prise from his fingers, and point it, and squeeze the trigger, and . . .

But it didn't happen.

Thinking about it all afterwards, Buffalo Arthur realised that it was the very fact that he was only seven, and slim at that, which had saved him. Because the rustler was so enormously fat that his giant stomach just sort of enfolded Buffalo Arthur like a great fleshy eiderdown, without the man, in his drunken sleep, even noticing this thin object pinned beneath him.

Buffalo Arthur noticed it all right, though. It must be like this if you're an ant, he thought, and someone has just trodden on you in bare feet. He resolved never to tread on an ant ever again.

He also resolved to get out from under the terrible weight. Worse even than the weight was the fact that the rustler's tied hands, still holding the gun, were pressing against his throat and slowly choking him to death. But he knew that if he did what he would have to do to shift the giant bulk, there was no way that the man would not wake up.

So it would all have to be done in a flash, everything timed right, everything perfect; it would be an all-or-nothing try, and if it went wrong, there was nothing to hope for but that the rustler was a good shot and would finish him off with his first bullet, quickly.

The gun was his main problem. So, inch by

tiny inch, he squirmed his hand up and under the gun, until his fingers were curled around the cold barrel. By the most amazing luck, his other arm, with the three lassoo-ends in it, was lying free outside the huge lump of rustler.

And with one hand on the rope-ends, and the other on the six-gun, Buffalo Arthur, seven years old and all alone, but brave as it is possible to be, started to count, to himself:

"One!" he counted.

"Two!" he counted.

"And ... THREE!" he yelled, and as he yelled, he sank his teeth into the great horny hand pressing on his mouth, and kicked upwards with all his remaining strength, and the rustler hurled himself onto his side, his fingers, even though their owner was still three-quarters asleep, automatically twitching for the trigger of his gun at just the very moment at which Buffalo Arthur was hurling it as far as he could into the darkness, and leaping up, and running into the night with the three rope-ends grasped in his small hand!

Now, you may know that if you wake up suddenly from a deep sleep to find yourself staring at a bright light, it takes some seconds to see anything at all, or, indeed, do anything at all. And since the three rustlers were coming not out of an ordinary sleep but out of a heavy drunken stupor, they all spent several seconds stumbling about, dazzled by the bright firelight, not realising why it was they could not move their hands, not really knowing where they were at all.

It wasn't, of course, very *many* seconds before they recovered, but it was just enough seconds for Buffalo Arthur and his master plan. For, having leapt off into the night, he made straight for the three closest animals, hurled himself at their feet, and slipped the Special Knot which he had prepared at the other end of the three lassoos over each of the thick forelegs.

He was just in time! As the third startled animal put down its foot again before it had realised what was going on, the ropes tautened with the frenzied pulling of the three rustlers, who by this time were roaring and cursing and tearing clumsily around the fire. And the more they pulled, the tighter grew the Special Knots.

And there was nothing at all that any of the rustlers could do about it when Buffalo

Arthur stood up, dusted himself down, thwacked the three animals across the rump with a large stick, and began moving the stolen herd out of the dark valley.

It was just after what would have been lunchtime, had they fancied any lunch (which they didn't), that Dan Dundee saw three cattle come out from behind that little hill I mentioned and wander slowly across the view from the cookhouse window. But he did not say anything, because it did not seem very important.

Then he saw five more. And after that, about a dozen. Then a whole herd, perhaps fifty animals.

"Look," he said, "promise you won't laugh, but all our cattle are supposed to be in the north range, aren't they?"

"So what?" said Billy Futt, who was thinking of poor little Buffalo Arthur and his orange carpet-bag.

"Well, where are all those coming from, then?"

They ran outside. The land between the knoll and the ranch-house was now so filled with lumbering, mooing cattle that not even a blade of grass could be seen. The three cowboys stared at them in disbelief.

At last, it dawned upon them.

"They're our lost cattle!" cried Dan Dundee.

"Of course," said a voice, behind him, low down.

The cowboys wheeled around.

It was Buffalo Arthur.

"But how . . . ?" shouted Billy Futt.

"But where . . . ?" cried Sam Sundown.

"But when . . . ?" roared Dan Dundee.

Buffalo Arthur smiled a secret smile.

"You can see a lot by moonlight," he said. "It's a good time to track rustlers. If you want a tip, that is."

Dan Dundee reeled back, amazed!

"But it's over a week since the cattle went," he exclaimed. "There have been winds, and other animals, and riders passing! All the tracks will have gone by now, blown away, trodden out!"

"Fat lot you know about tracking," replied Buffalo Arthur. "When you get 264 cattle on the move, they tread down bushes, snap

branches, trample river banks. You can follow them clear as anything, by moonlight."

"But why go by night at all?" asked Billy Futt. "Surely day would be even better?"

Buffalo Arthur smiled his smile again.

"Fat lot you know about rustlers!" he told Billy Futt. "By day, those rustlers would have seen my horse's dust from *miles* away! And of course," he added, in a voice that made Billy Futt break out in goose-pimples, "they would have been awake when I caught up with them."

The cowboys' eyes grew as round as dinner-plates and almost as large. They stared at Buffalo Arthur! They goggled at each other!

"Caught *up* with them?" croaked Dan Dundee, as soon as he could manage to make the words come out. "You mean you didn't just find the cattle wandering about?"

Buffalo Arthur cleared his throat, and tried

not to look too pleased with himself, because he knew that was not the thing at all.

"About ten miles from here," he said, "there is a little green gully, hidden away in a sort of pocket between two hills . . ."

"I know the place," breathed Sam Sundown, "it's – "

"Shut up!" snapped Dan Dundee. "Go on, Buffalo Arthur."

"Thank you. It was clear to me," continued Buffalo Arthur, "that the rustlers' plan was to keep your cattle there until the coast was clear and the fuss had died down, before changing their brands and moving them on. Like all simple plans," and here Buffalo Arthur looked at them very wisely indeed, "it was a pretty good one."

"You're right there!" said Dan Dundee.

"How would *you* know?" Billy Futt asked him, rather rudely.

Sam Sundown drew his gun, and checked it, and spun the barrel, the way you're supposed to when looking for rustlers, or similar.

"Ten miles away, eh?" he said, in the bravest voice he could find. "And that's where they are now, is it?"

For the third (and the last) time, Buffalo Arthur gave his special smile.

"Oh, no," he said, "not now."

And he turned, and he looked, and the

three cowboys looked where he looked, and over the hill came the last three cattle (the 262nd, the 263rd, and the 264th).

And to each animal, a rope was attached, by the very special non-slip knot that Buffalo Arthur himself had invented. And at the other end of each rope, a rustler stumbled, his hands bound in front of him; and on the face of each one, as you can probably imagine, was an expression so horrible that you'll have to imagine that, too, because I can't possibly bring myself to describe it.

And as for the three cowboys, they had to hold on to one another to keep from falling down in amazement!

"But – but – but HOW?" cried Dan Dundee. "You're a *kid*!"

"He's a *kid*!" exclaimed Billy Futt, mainly to the sky.

"Just a *kid*!" gasped Sam Sundown, mainly to the hills.

Buffalo Arthur looked at them in a private way, not offended, just sort of, well, slightly amused. It was a look he reserved for grown-ups in certain circumstances. He had used it quite often, as a matter of fact.

"What you forget," he explained, "is that it was night-time. That was all part of my plan. I just crept up on them while they slept, and I tied their hands together ever so carefully with my special knots, and I tied the other end of the rope to the biggest three animals I could find. Then I just prodded the animals with a sharp stick, and we all moved out!"

"A sharp stick!" shrieked the largest and nastiest-looking rustler, whose terrible face (poking up from the herd of nearby cattle) was all that could be seen of him. "Not even a gun! And I, Filthy Sid Mullett, am the quickest draw west of the Oklahoma Kid!"

"And *I'm* the Oklahoma Kid!" moaned another voice, somewhat muffled by the cow

that was sitting on him.

"You don't need a gun," said Buffalo Arthur, "when you use your brains."

Dan Dundee shook his head in astonishment.

"And none of them even heard you moving about?" he said.

"I'm very light on my feet," said Buffalo Arthur. He looked very sternly at Dan Dundee, and Billy Futt, and Sam Sundown. "It's probably because I'm only seven," he said.

And after that, there really was nothing more to say.